# Lola
## Knows a Lot

For Sasha and Sophie
—J.M.

To Marisa and Pablo
—S.P.

Balzer + Bray is an imprint of HarperCollins Publishers.

Lola Knows a Lot
Text copyright © 2016 by Jenna McCarthy
Illustrations copyright © 2016 by Sara Palacios
All rights reserved. Manufactured in China.

Library of Congress Cataloging-in-Publication Data
McCarthy, Jenna
  Lola knows a lot / written by Jenna McCarthy ; illustrated by Sara Palacios.
 — First edition.
  pages  cm
  Summary: Lola, who knows a lot, worries when her big sister, Charlotte, tells
her that everyone at school will know more than she does, but when their mother
suggests she list all her areas of expertise, Lola realizes that one important thing
she knows is that she is ready to learn more.
  ISBN 978-0-06-225017-9 (hardcover)
  [1. Learning—Fiction. 2. Family life—Fiction. 3. First day of school—Fiction.
4. Humorous stories.] I. Palacios, Sara, illustrator. II. Title.
PZ7.1.M42Lol 2016                                                    2014041058
[E]—dc23                                                                  CIP
                                                                          AC

The artist used watercolor, colored pencils, cut paper, and digital media to create
the digital illustrations for this book.
Typography by Carla Weise
16  17  18  19  20   SCP   10  9  8  7  6  5  4  3  2  1
❖
First Edition

# Lola
## Knows a Lot

days till school starts
10 9 8 7 6
5 4 3 2
①

written by Jenna McCarthy          illustrated by Sara Palacios

BALZER + BRAY
An Imprint of HarperCollinsPublishers

I don't know how I know all the things I know, but trust me, I know a lot.

Not to brag or anything, but I know how
to do a perfect cartwheel, count to ten in
Spanish, and hula-hoop with my eyes closed.

I know how to grow giant sunflowers and catch tiny lizards and tie my own shoes.

Yup, I am *totally* ready for school.

At least I thought I was. Until my big sister, Charlotte, had to ask:

"Can you write your name in cursive?

Count to one hundred by fives?

Name all the planets?

Find Mexico on a map?"

She says everyone at school is going to know more than I do. What if she's right?

Mom says to ignore Charlotte. (She says that a lot.)

"Think of all the things you already know!" Mom adds.
"I'll bet you could make a pretty big list."

I am good at making lists.
Let's see. . . .

I know how to make my bed.
I'm even better at it than Charlotte.

I even know how to drive a car . . .
from the backseat anyway.

"The light is green, Mom," I tell her.
"That means you can go!"

I'm practically an expert with the remote control.

"If you want to pause it, you press this button,"
I explain for the millionth time.

My mom is still learning.

I know stuff even my dad doesn't know!
(He's not always happy about this.)

"Dad," I ask, "are spiders insects?"
"I believe they are," Dad says.
"Actually, they're not," I tell him.
"They're arachnids."

I'm good at driving my sister crazy.

I'm not saying you should try it. I'm just saying I happen to be especially good at it.

I know that practicing isn't as fun as doing.

But I also know you can't get good at
anything without a lot of practice.

I know that your mom gets really, really supermad when you cut your own hair.

You might want to trust me on that one.

I'm great at playing the piano.

"Not 'Chopsticks' again," says Charlotte.
"Please, anything but 'Chopsticks.'"

And I never even took lessons!

I know that it's not always easy being the little sister.

But sometimes having a big sister can be pretty nice.

I know it's important to be honest. That's why I never, ever tell a lie.

"What are we doing today?" I ask Mom.
"You're going over to Piper's house to play."
"But I want to stay home and bug Charlotte and her friends!"

I know that you have to eat your vegetables.

"Where would you like your broccoli?" Mom asks.
"Nowhere, please," I tell her.

Knowing it and liking it are two different things.

I don't always know where I put all my things.

"Mom!" I call. "Have you seen my sparkly pink headband?"
"Did you try looking on top of your head?" Mom suggests.

But I know that finding them feels really good.

I know "The Star-Spangled Banner" by heart.

"And the rocking red glare,

thunder bursting in there . . ."

Well, sort of.

I know what I want to be when I grow up.

"When I grow up,
I'm going to be a ballerina.

Or a dolphin trainer.

Or an astronaut.

Or an artist.

Or a butterfly...."

I guess I'm still working on that one.

And I know that getting out of bed
in the morning isn't always easy.

Mom says you have
to get dressed or
we'll be late.

At least for some people.

I may not know *everything* yet . . .

but I know I'm ready to learn
all the things I still don't know.